Supersnouts!

by STEVE BJÖRKMAN

Holiday House / New York

Printed in the United States of America

The text typeface is Soupbone.

The artwork was painted with ink and watercolor.

www.holidayhouse.com

First Edition

1 3 5 7 9 10 8 6 4 2

Library of Congress Cataloging-in-Publication Data

Björkman, Steve.

Supersnouts! / by Steve Björkman.—1st ed.

p. cm.

Summary: Hamlet the piglet joins Snoutbuster and Kernel Hog

in a flying confrontation with two burglars on Farmer Frank's farm.

ISBN 0-8234-1810-3 (hardcover)

[1. Heroes—Fiction. 2. Pigs—Fiction. 3. Robbers and outlaws—Fiction.

4. Farm life—Fiction.] I. Title.

PZ7.B528615Su 2004

[E]—dc22

2003050923

For David,
my "rascal pig with rebel ways."
Thank you for your inspiration.
—S. B.

It was a quiet, peaceful farmyard evening, right? Wrong! Oh yes, Snoutbuster and Kernel Hog were snoring. But while other piglets curled up close to their moms, Hamlet snuff—snuffled the breeze and peered into the distance.

"Something's rotten in the state of Denmark," he whispered.

"We're in the state of Iowa," muttered Kernel Hog. "Go back to sleep, runt."

"Someone's creeping around the farmhouse."

Kernel Hog yawned. "It's just Farmer Frank taking a stroll with his wife."

"Do Farmer Frank and his wife wear black masks while strolling?" Hamlet asked.

"Not unless it's Halloween."

Shoutbuster and Kernel Hog swung their snouts and stared.

Hamlet's eyes got wide. "So it's true, isn't it? You're the Superhero Pig Patrol, Hooves of Steel, and Snoutmasters of Glory! I've heard the stories."

Snoutbuster pulled a sack from under the trough and ripped it open. He adjusted his goggles while Kernel Hog tugged on his tights. With a nod from Snoutbuster, Kernel Hog grumbled, "Yes, Hamlet, the stories are all true."

"Jumpin' hog jowls! What do I wear?" Hamlet asked.

"You're staying right here," Kernel Hog said.

"But you just gotta let me come!"

Kernel Hog looked at Hamlet's pleading eyes. "Oh, all right, but this will be on-the-hoof training. Gear up. You can use my old rocket pack."

He's more of a Boy Snout than a superhero.

Hamlet hauled his hooves to find something to wear.
It wasn't yellow SPAM™-dex, but it would work.

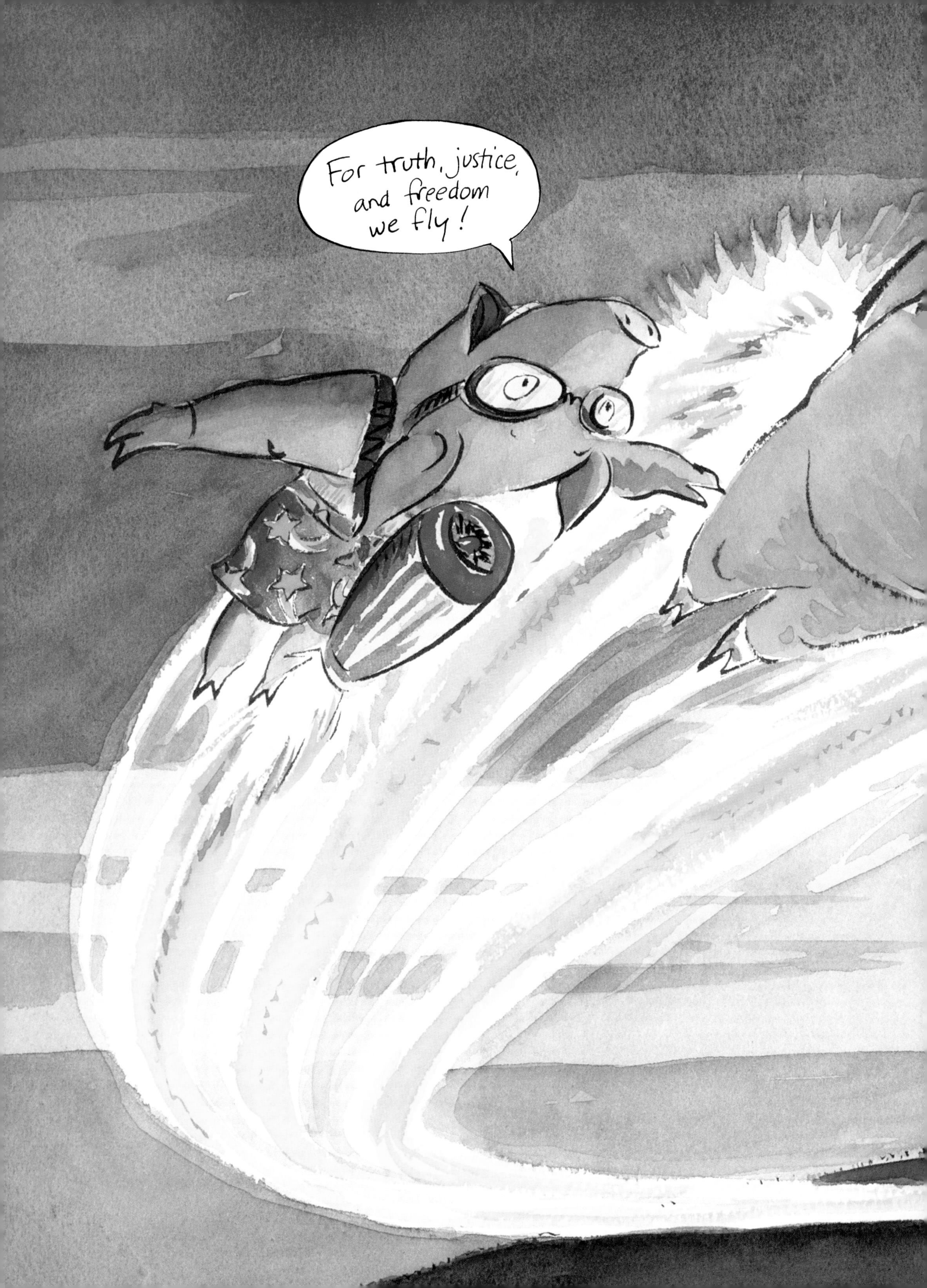
For truth, justice, and freedom we fly!

The three raised pigs' feet toward the sky.
   Ripping a fiery swath through the night, they were
on their way to fame, glory, and maybe a nice mud
bath when it was all over.

The two farmyard villains crept across the porch and through Farmer Frank's window. They couldn't hear the swoosh of three fine swine fliers. They couldn't see Hamlet's brighty tighties or the determined stares of Pork with a Purpose. And if they could have seen them, they wouldn't have believed their eyes anyway!

"Hurry up! I can't hold this forever!" one burglar grumbled.

"You're always grabbing the big stuff! Next time don't be such a hog!" the other hissed.

"Okay, boys, let's take the leap to hyper-hog speed and hit 'em from the flanks. Break!"

Kernel Hog and Snoutbuster spun off to the left and right, but Hamlet didn't have a clue as to what they were talking about. He decided to stay close to Kernel Hog. A little too close.

His rocket blast knocked the Kernel right into
the trash cans. It wasn't pretty.
The villains tied up Kernel Hog in a burglar knot.

"Oh yeah?" cried Hamlet. "This is one show that's about to be canceled!"

He pulled the rocket lever and pushed the red button at the same time. It was a pigheaded thing to do. Hamlet spiraled through the trees, bounced through the begonias, and plowed through the picket fence.

Haieeeeeeeee

Yikes!

The flashlights flew. The pickets poked.
The littlest power porker tripped, slipped,
and sprawled across the porch, picking up
splinters in his hams along the way.
Hamlet squealed as if he was a pork-fu
karate master . . . in pain.

eeyah!

It's a flying swinesaucer!

Glory Hog.

Hamlet captured the burglars and stood triumphant,
a dizzy superhero on the lawn.
    Snoutbuster powered down to untie the Kernel.

The old hams hog–tied the burglars, stacked up the stolen stuff, and congratulated each other with high hooves.

Singing like a pork–belly choir, they were in hog heaven as they hoofed it back to the yard.

Hamlet, maybe someday you'll work for the Federal Pigpen of Investigation.

The FPI? Really?

The next morning the police picked up the two burglars, who confessed to everything. They even told strange stories Farmer Frank and the police found quite unbelievable. Superhero pigs? Jet-powered porkers? These goofs must be crazy!

"The only thing I can't understand," said Farmer Frank to his wife, "is all these little hoofprints. Do you think it's possible that what the burglars said was true?"

She shook her head at him and laughed.
"When pigs fly, Frank. When pigs fly."